Ask your booksellers for other books in *The Rumpoles and the Barleys* series by Karen Mezek.

The Rumpoles and the Barleys
A Picnic with the Barleys

THE RUMPOLES AND THE BARLEYS

Library of Congress Cataloging-in-Publication Data

Mezek, Karen, 1956-
  The Rumpoles and the Barleys.

  Summary: Two little mice who live in a grand home learn to be more thankful for what they have after a misadventure takes them far from home, among a more modest family of mice who live underground near a barley field.
  [1. Mice—Fiction]   I. Title.
PZ7.M5748Ru   1988   [E]   88-80376
ISBN 0-89081-657-3

Copyright © 1988 by Karen Mezek
Published by Harvest House Publishers
Eugene, Oregon 97402

Printed and bound in Singapore by Tien Wah Press (PTE) Ltd.

The Rumpoles
and
The Barleys

by Karen Mezek

For Katya

Harvest House Publishers
Eugene, Oregon 97402

Once there was a family of mice who lived in the attic of the old Rumpole Mansion on the edge of Dilbury Town. They were, of course, very proud to live in such a fine house and were pleased to be known as "the Rumpole Mice."

Today was Saturday and the two little mouse children,
Eustace and Prunella, were so-ooo excited.

Downstairs a grand party was in progress and their tiny noses twitched and sniffed the wonderful smells that filled their attic home.

Papa Rumpole kept scurrying back and forth to the dining room, bringing home yummy bits of crisp chicken, apple stuffing, mashed potatoes, gravy, carrots, peas, parsnips . . .

. . . strawberry tarts, chocolate mints, and, of course, a fine selection of cheeses.

Naturally, he was careful to avoid Samuel the cat. One could never
tell if he was really asleep or just pretending.

When all the delicious tidbits had been collected and laid out on Mama's very best tablecloth, the Rumpole mice sat down to dinner.

Sad to say, Eustace and Prunella were rather spoiled. Not only did they forget their manners, but they immediately began their usual table conversation . . .

"I don't like parsnips," pouted Prunella.

"She has more stuffing than I do," whined Eustace.

". . . and I just want dessert!" yelled Prunella.

"Children, children," cried their mother. "Do be good—and thankful for what you have. Some poor mice are starving."

Eustace banged his elbows on the table, upsetting the gravy all over the clean cloth.

"That will do. Upstairs to bed at once!" ordered Papa Rumpole. "And nothing to eat until breakfast," he added.

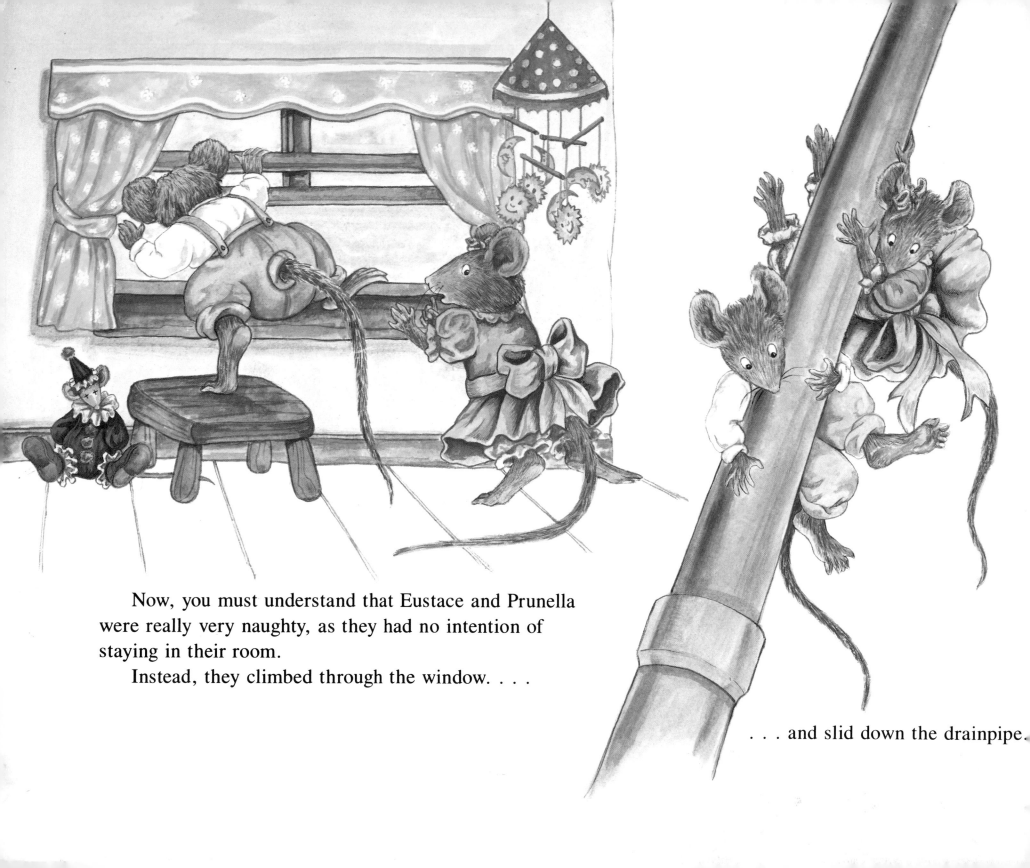

Now, you must understand that Eustace and Prunella were really very naughty, as they had no intention of staying in their room.

Instead, they climbed through the window. . . .

. . . and slid down the drainpipe.

"Watch out!" squeaked Prunella when she noticed Samuel asleep on the windowsill below.

The cat opened his green eyes wide, but before he could quite wake up, the two runaways had jumped right over his head and into a passing farm wagon.

Kersplat! Too late Eustace and Prunella realized the wagon was fu[ll]
of rotten fruit and vegetables. They tried to climb out of the squashy,
gooey, smelly mess, but it was impossible. Helplessly, they watched th[e]
Rumpole Mansion disappear further and further into the distance.

After a very long while the wagon stopped, and before they knew what was happening, they were dumped onto an even bigger pile of rotten, smelly stuff. Down they tumbled in a tangle of potato peels, melon rinds and stale bread crusts. Unfortunately, the empty wagon was already heading back and their short little legs could not run fast enough to catch it.

The next moment Eustace and Prunella became aware of a brown mouse with beady eyes and a pair of very long whiskers peeking over a log.

"G'd afternoon," the mouse said in a jaunty manner. "What have we here?"

"We fell into a wagon full of rotten old vegetables!" they both squeaked at once.

"And we're lost," Prunella added, sniffing and blowing her nose.

"Well, well! That's a fine mess," said the brown mouse as he hopped over the log. "I'm Dagwood Barley, at your service. Lucky for you I happened to be passing by."

Ordinarily, Eustace and Prunella would not have talked to such a common field mouse, but they were overjoyed when he offered to take them home to his mama and papa.

The Barley family lived in a modest hole on the edge of a barley field. Never having been in such humble surroundings, Prunella made a terrible fuss. She twitched her nose in disgust and declared, "I'm not going down there in the dark!"

Eustace solved the problem by giving her a good push.

". . . Oooh," squeaked Prunella as she rolled down
and bumped into the front door.

Once inside, they were surprised to find themselves in a cheery house, overflowing with noisy mice.

"Oh, you poor dears!" cried Mama Barley when Dagwood had introduced the children. She bustled them off to the bathroom immediately for a good wash and change of clothes.

"Dinner time!" shouted Dagwood, who was feeling quite important.
Everyone stopped what they were doing at once and hurried to the table.

There was a good deal of chair scraping and rearranging, but somehow everyone managed to squeeze in.

Papa Barley rapped on the table for quiet. Eustace and Prunella had already grabbed their milk mugs but quickly put them down again. Papa waited until all the little Barleys—Eustace and Prunella too—had bowed their heads and closed their eyes. Then he gave thanks for the food.

My, how good it tasted! Eustace and Prunella ate every bite on their plates—even their vegetables. Mama Barley beamed with pleasure when they asked for more and remembered to say "please" and "thank you."

After dinner Papa Barley opened a big black book, almost as big as he was. When he read "In everything give thanks" Prunella looked around the room. Everyone seemed so happy—and thankful. But she was suddenly miserable.

A big tear splashed down on her lap. "I'm so dreadfully ashamed of myself," she sniffled. "I've been so unthankful."

"Me too," spluttered Eustace. "And so selfish."

"It's hard to be miserable when you're thankful," said Mama Barley.
"Why not think of things you can give thanks for?"

Prunella thought for just a moment.
"New friends," she smiled.
"A cozy home in a barley field," added Eustace.
"Mama and Papa," they both said together.

"Peas!"

"Parsnips!"

"Patches on our clothes!"

"Even yucky wagons!"

"Time for bed," announced Papa Barley. "It's been a long day. We'll have to get up early and take you home so your Mama and Papa won't worry."

The next morning all the Barleys came along for the trip back to the Rumpole Mansion. Up they hopped into the same old wagon, only this time it seemed a grand way to travel with their new friends.

Soon their own dear home came into view. "Good-bye, good-bye," they called as they climbed the old familiar drainpipe.

They had just hopped in through their bedroom window when Mama Rumpole knocked on the door.

"Time to get up," she called. "And I do hope you've learned a lesson."

"Oh yes," Eustace and Prunella answered, smiling
to each other. "We have."

"O give thanks unto the Lord for He is good."

Psalm 118:1